For Everyone to Share

For Amy, Daniel and Kate
G.L.

For my beautiful daughter Chloe
D.H.

First published in Great Britain in 2008 by Gullane Children's Books.
This paperback edition published in 2009 by

Gullane Children's Books

185 Fleet Street, London, EC4A 2HS
www.gullanebooks.com

3   5   7   9   10   8   6   4   2

Text © Gillian Lobel 2008
Illustrations © Daniel Howarth 2008

The right of Gillian Lobel and Daniel Howarth to be identified as the author and illustrator of
this work has been asserted by them in accordance with the Copyright, Designs and Patents Act, 1988.

A CIP record for this title is available from the British Library.

ISBN 978-1-86233-748-0

Printed and bound in China

For Everyone to Share

Gillian Lobel • Daniel Howarth

Little Mouse was fast asleep in his soft, cosy nest.
It was so warm, snuggled next to his mother and his six
brothers and sisters. Suddenly his nose tickled ...

"Achoo!" said Little Mouse.

He did a big stretch, from his tiny pink nose,
to his long curly tail. Little Mouse scrambled
out of his nest. All around him was dark and
dim. But, far away, he saw something
different. Something that made
his eyes water for a moment.

What was it?

Little Mouse pattered
along a leafy tunnel.
Strange smells tickled his
nose. His whiskers quivered
with excitement.

And suddenly he was there – there in the big brightness.

Curiously he tiptoed into the daylight . . .

And he saw – a tiny fat person, dressed in a furry coat of
black and gold! He zizzed loudly in Little Mouse's ears.
"Who are you?" cried Little Mouse.
"Please tell me your name!"
The furry person zizzed even louder.
"I'm a **bee**, Little Mouse!"
And he flew away and . . .

landed on something
yellow and shining.
"Don't go," squeaked Little Mouse.
"Please tell me what you're sitting on!"

"This is a **flower**, Little Mouse," zizzed the bee.
And he climbed right into the heart of the flower, to sip his breakfast.
"Bee, flower," murmured Little Mouse. "What a wonderful place this is!"

He felt something soft and lovely on his back,
and lifted his eyes. Far, far above him was a glowing ring
of light! It shone on his ears and toes, and warmed them.
"Please tell me, Buzzy Bee, who is that?"
Little Mouse pointed high into the sky.

"That's the **sun**, Little Mouse – the blessed sun!
And she lives in the **bright blue sky**."
"Bee, flower, sun and bright blue sky," murmured
Little Mouse. "And what is that, Buzzy Bee, please tell me ..."

But Buzzy Bee had zizzed away.

Just then, something floated past Little Mouse's nose and landed
right next to him. She was as blue as the sky, and lighter than the air.
"Oh Little Sky," he gasped. "Please tell me who you are."
"I am a **butterfly**, Little Mouse," she breathed,
and a silvery laugh rippled over the flowers.

"Bee, flower, sun,
sky and butterfly,"
murmured Little Mouse.
"How wonderful this place is!"

"And there is even more," said the butterfly. "Look!"
And she showed him the birds, who filled the air with music, the whispering grasses, starry daisies, and the dewdrops on a spider's web.

"And now I must go," said the blue butterfly.
"Goodbye, Little Mouse!" And up and away she fluttered.

Little Mouse trembled with excitement.
"I will go home, and tell everyone what I have seen!"

But Mummy Mouse was already looking out for him.

"Mummy, Mummy!" called Little Mouse joyfully. "I have seen so
many things here in the big outside – a buzzy bee, a flower,
the golden sun, the bright blue sky, a butterfly,
the birds of the air – oh, so much. What is this place,
Mummy? Please tell me, I want to know!"

"Why, this is the **world**, Little Mouse – the beautiful world!" laughed his mother.

And they trotted home happily together.

"The world . . ." murmured Little Mouse, as he
snuggled into his mother's arms. "The big, beautiful world.
But who is it for, Mummy? Is it a world for us?"

"Yes," smiled his mother. "It is a world for bees, and butterflies,
and flowers, for birds and spiders and grasses that sing.
And it's a world for us too — it's a world . . .

for everyone to share!"

Then Little Mouse gave a deep and happy sigh,
curled up into his sweet, warm nest with his six
brothers and sisters, and fell fast asleep.